This book is to be returned on or b
the last date stamped below.

THIS WALKER BOOK BELONGS TO:

———————————————————

———————————————————

———————————————————

———————————————————

To Joe
S. M.

For Rachel
I. B.

First published 1996 by Walker Books Ltd
87 Vauxhall Walk, London SE11 5HJ

This edition published 2001

2 4 6 8 10 9 7 5 3 1

Text © 1996 Sam McBratney
Illustrations © 1996 Ivan Bates

The right of Sam McBratney to be identified as author
of this work has been asserted by him in accordance
with the Copyright, Designs and Patents Act 1988

Printed in Hong Kong

British Library Cataloguing in Publication Data:
a catalogue record for this book
is available from the British Library

ISBN 0-7445-7837-X

JUST ONE!

Written by Sam McBratney
Illustrated by Ivan Bates

WALKER BOOKS

AND SUBSIDIARIES

LONDON • BOSTON • SYDNEY

Down in the woods, little Digger was picking blackberries with the old, grey squirrel who looked after him.
They picked blackberries along by the river, and they picked them in the shady lane.
Soon they had a big pile of blackberries.

"Is this the biggest pile of blackberries you've ever seen?" said little Digger to Old-and-Grey.

"Yes it is," replied Old-and-Grey.

"I'll go and look for something to put them in, or we'll never carry them home."

"Will I be in charge of our blackberries while you're away?" asked Digger.

"Yes. But don't eat too many – just a few," said Old-and-Grey.

And off he went to find something to put the blackberries in.

A country mouse ran out of the cornfield at the edge of the woods. She sat down beside Digger and the pile of blackberries.
"I'm in charge of all these," said Digger.
"They look lovely," said the mouse.
"Do you think I could have some?"
"Well, don't eat too many," said Digger.
"Just a few."

The country mouse ate some of the blackberries, and so did little Digger.

A flat-footed duck waddled up from the
river. He looked at Digger, and the
country mouse, and then he pointed
his beak at the pile of blackberries.
"Very nice indeed," said the duck.
"I'm in charge of them," said Digger.
"Do you think I could have some?"
asked the duck.
"Well, not too many,"
said Digger.
"Just a few."

The flat-footed duck ate some of the
blackberries, and so did Digger and
the country mouse.

Then a bouncy baby rabbit came out of the woods. She hopped right round the blackberries and sat down beside Digger, and the duck, and the country mouse. "Do you think I could taste some of those lovely blackberries?" she said. "Well, not too many," said Digger. "You can just have a few."

The bouncy baby rabbit ate some of the blackberries, and so did Digger and the duck and the country mouse.

Then they heard the noise of
someone approaching through the
woods. Old-and-Grey was coming back
with something to hold the blackberries.

"I hope there won't be too many to carry in this," he said as he came closer.
"No," said Digger, looking at the pile of blackberries. "Not too many…"

"Just one!"

SAM MCBRATNEY says of *Just One*, "This story reminds me of the times when, as a child, I ate myself into trouble. Perhaps a biscuit disappeared, or the last of the cream – somehow my mother always knew where to look for the guilty party. In *Just One*, little Digger doesn't mean to be greedy, but when you have hungry friends too, it's amazing how quickly a lot of blackberries can turn into almost none!"

Sam has written many books for children including *Guess How Much I Love You*, which has sold more than ten million copies worldwide and was voted children's book of the year by American booksellers. Married with three grown-up children, he lives in County Antrim, Northern Ireland.

IVAN BATES says that "drawing little Digger was wonderful fun, particularly showing him trying to hold on to his dignity but always giving in to the yummy temptation. You can't really blame him – I don't think I'd be able to resist eating those lovely blackberries either!"

Ivan studied Illustration at Manchester Polytechnic, and decided to concentrate on illustrating for children after falling in love with the line-work of artists such as Tenniel and Ardizzone. He has illustrated three other Sam McBratney titles: *Just You and Me*, *In Crack Willow Wood* and *The Dark at the Top of the Stairs*. He lives in Norfolk.